DIARY

MINECRAFT ZOMBIE

Book 11

by Zack Zombie

Saturday

"**Y**OU'RE THE WORST!"

SLAM!

Urrrrgggghhhhh!

Why do parents have to be so mean!

All I wanted to do was stay up and join the "All Day Minecraft Marathon PVP Video Game Tournament" like all the other famous Ztubers.

But noooooooooo!

"You're only 13 years old, blah, blah, blah!" they said.

"And you need your sleep if you want to grow up to be an unhealthy young zombie, blah, blah, blah!"

"Don't you know that if you don't sleep you won't grow any spores, molds and fungus? Blah, blah, blah."

"Eat your Mushroom stew, blah, blah, blah!"

"Dirty your room, blah, blah, blah!"

"Pick your scabs, blah, blah, blah!"

"Pick up your butt, blah, blah, blah!"

Sometimes I wonder if you have to pass a "mean" test to be a parent.

And only the really mean ones can have more than one kid.

My parents must've gotten an A++++ on their "Meanness" exam.

With extra points for nagging, hovering, lecturing and bugging.

Knowing my parents, they probably went to a "Meanness" boot camp to prepare for their Meanness exam.

That's probably where they learned how to say no to everything.

Drill Instructor: "SOLDIER! WHAT DID YOU SAY?!!

Mom and Dad: "YES SIRR!"

Drill Instructor: "WHAT WAS THAT?!!"

Mom and Dad: "I MEAN, NO SIR!"

Drill Instructor: "AND WHAT DO WE SAY NO TO, SOLDIER?!!"

Mom and Dad: "EVERYTHING THE KID THINKS IS FUN, SIR!"

Drill Instructor: "LIKE WHAT, SOLDIER?!!"

Mom and Dad: "LIKE VIDEO GAMES, SWEETS BEFORE DINNER, AND STAYING UP LATE, SIR!"

Drill Instructor: "AND WHAT IS OUR MOTTO AS PARENTS, SOLDIER?!!"

Mom and Dad: "SAY NO TO FUN, SAY NO TO CAKE, SAY NO TO GAMES, AND STAYING UP LATE, SIR!"

Drill Instructor: "ARE YOU SURE, SOLDIER?!!"

Mom and Dad: "SIR! YES, SIR!"

Drill Instructor: "WHAT WAS THAT?!!"

Mom and Dad: "I MEAN, SIR! NO SIR!"

Drill Instructor: "SAY IT AGAIN, SOLDIER!!!!"

Mom and Dad: "JUST SAY NO TO EVERYTHING THE KID LIKES, SIR!"

Yeah, that's probably where they learned it.

Man, being a thirteen year old zombie really stinks.

Sunday

I bet Steve knows how to deal with parents.

That's because Steve doesn't live with his parents. He lives with villagers.

He probably traded in his parents years ago.

Yeah, villagers like to trade. He probably got an emerald for them.

Man, if he could teach me how to do that, that would be awesome.

Well, just for at least a few days anyway. Then I could enter the next All Day Minecraft Marathon PVP Tournament that's happening this week.

I went to go find Steve, but he wasn't at his house.

I went to his favorite punching tree, but he wasn't there either.

He wasn't at his diamond cave either.

I wonder where he could be.

All of a sudden I heard, "OOOOOHHHHHMMMM, OOOOOHHHHHMMMM."

I followed it to the middle of the forest, and there was Steve.

But he was standing on his head making noises…

"OOOOOHHHHHMMMM. OOOOOHHHHHMMMM."

"Yo, Steve, watcha doing, man?"

"Oh, hey Zombie. Whaddup Dawg?"

7

"What dog?"

"You dawg."

"Whose dog?"

"You dawg."

I think Steve was standing on his head too long. He thinks I'm a dog.

"Dude, what dog?"

"Forget it, dawg," Steve said as he got back on his feet. "Sup Zombie, how's it going?"

"Uh, OK. Hey, why were you on your head making those strange noises? You sounded like my uncle Rufus when he lost his jawbone."

"Oh that? That was Yoga."

"Yogurt?"

"Not yogurt. Yoga."

"Yoda?"

"Yo-Ga!"

"What's Yo-ga?"

"Yoga is something you do to help you find inner peace," Steve said.

"Oh, I lost an inner piece once. I think it was a piece of my spinal column… Man that hurt. I think it slipped out and got lodged in my butt."

Steve just looked at me with a strange look.

"What inner piece did you lose?" I asked. "Oh, I get it; standing on your head probably helped you get it out of your butt, right?"

"No, not that kind of inner piece. Inner peace."

Now I looked at Steve with a strange look. *Maybe the piece is still stuck in his butt,* I thought.

"Does it hurt, Steve?"

Steve took his hand and slapped himself in the face. *I guess humans have to slap themselves to get the inner piece outta their butts.*

"Zombie, sometimes when you're feeling some really strong feelings, you have to find a way of getting them out."

"Out of your butt?"

Steve slapped himself again. *Man, that thing must be really stuck in there.*

"No, Zombie. Out of your heart. You need to get your feelings out of your heart."

"What's a heart?"

Steve gave me another weird look.

"Wait a minute, you don't have a heart?" he asked.

"I don't know. I've never really heard that word before."

"Well, let's take a look. Lift up your shirt."

I lifted up my shirt, and started to giggle when Steve stuck his hand in the hole in my stomach.

Next thing you know, his whole arm was in there feeling around for something. All of a

11

sudden his fingers started poking out of my nose socket.

Then he pulled his arm out.

"Yup, no heart. Wow, Zombie, that's crazy. But, then…where do your feelings come from?"

"What are feelings?" I asked him.

"Feelings are those things that make you happy, sad, afraid or embarrassed."

"I thought farting did that."

"Well…yeah. But I mean when you're not farting."

That's a good question. Where do my feelings come from?

"I don't know," I said.

Steve looked at me kind of serious this time.

"What is it?" I asked him.

"Well, then what do you do when your feelings get really intense? How do you calm down?"

"You mean without using yogurt?"

"Uh… Yeah."

Man, Steve was asking some really hard questions. Where do my feelings come from? What do I do when my feelings get too intense? What flavor yogurt I like? I was getting really confused.

"Steve, why should I care about this stuff?"

"Because one day you're going to have some really intense feelings, and if you don't know what to do with them, strange things could start happening to you."

I said goodbye to Steve and I went home. As I was walking away, I could hear him start moaning again like before.

I guess he's trying to find that inner piece again.

What was it that I needed to ask Steve about again?

Man, I totally forgot.

But talking about yogurt really made me hungry.

Monday

"**M**om! MOOOOOMMMMMMMMM!!!!!!"

"What is it, dear?!!!!"

My mom ran into my room.

"Look at my face!"

"Oh dear."

"FRANCIS!" my mom yelled.

"What is it Mildred?" my dad asked, running into my room.

"Dad, look at my face!"

"Oh, boy."

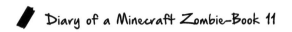
I could tell by looking at my Mom and Dad's faces that they knew what was going on with me.

"WHAT'S HAPPENING TO ME?!!!"

I looked at the mirror again, and my face was as red as an apple.

"It's called mood skin, honey," my mom said.

"Mood skin?!!! What's that?"

"Well, Zombie… It happens during puberty, when you have a lot of really intense emotions that you're feeling," Mom said. "If you don't find a way to release those feelings, well…strange things start to happen with your body."

"Has this ever happened to you, Mom?"

"Not to me, but I think your father went through something like that, right Francis?"

"DAD!!!! DO SOMETHING!"

16

"Well, Zombie, there's not much you can do. You just have to wait till it goes away," Dad said.

"How long did you have to wait?"

All of sudden my Dad started to rub his arm. Then he started to roll up his sleeve. About halfway up his arm, his green skin turned neon yellow.

"Well, remember I told you that I got this yellow spot from an accident at my job at the Nuclear Power Plant... Well, I wasn't being totally honest with you..."

"Wha..?!!!!"

"Well, it's almost totally gone. I think after the 20th year, that's when it really started to fade..."

"WHHAATTTT!!!!! I start school next week. I can't go to school like this!"

All of a sudden my skin started to glow a really bright red.

SHHIINNNEE!!*

"Whoa, Zombie! Calm down. Don't worry, son, we'll take you to the doctor tomorrow. I'm sure they have a cure for mood skin now. They've made a lot of advances in medicine since your Father's day."

"Hey!" Dad said.

"Sorry, dear," Mom said with a smirk on her face.

Oh man, my young 13 year old Zombie life is ruined! If I go to school like this, I'll be laughed out of middle school.

Yeah, I'm still in middle school by the way. Even though I'm going to the 9th grade.

Man, just when I was really excited about going to high school, they announced that they were adding a 9th grade to our school.

I think Rajit's Dad pulled some strings because he wanted Rajit to stay with his friends in middle school. Since all of us were graduating, he didn't want Rajit to be alone. Next thing you know, we have a 9th grade in our middle school.

Man, being a Kajillionaire...or I guess a Rajitionaire... must be so awesome.

But it's probably better this way.

I don't think I was ready for high school.

You see, all of the other guys have gotten bigger, but I haven't grown that much. I'm still the shortest one out of all of them.

Actually, I think I'm the shortest kid out of all the mob kids at school.

I'm even shorter than Blake, the Guardian, even when he flops over on his side.

But, thank goodness for Rajit. I'm still bigger than he is.

So I hang out with Rajit a lot...

Especially in front of the girls.

And I'm really glad I'm not going to high school looking like this. First day of school I'd be laughed out of town.

I mean, who ever heard of a red faced zombie?

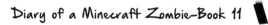

21

Tuesday

"**M**ommy, look!"

I hoped the little kid wasn't talking about me.

"Dear, it's not polite to point," the zombie lady said to her son in the Doctor's office.

"But he looks like a lollipop."

Yup. He was.

"Honey, SHHHH! It's not nice to make fun of the young Mooshroom. They have feelings too you know."

All of a sudden my face started to glow a bright red.

My mom took her green nylon stocking and put it over my head. I guess she thought it would help.

It didn't.

Everybody in the waiting area ran for their lives.

"OK, now who's next?" the doctor asked walking into the waiting room. "Hey, where'd everybody go?"

"We're next, Doctor," my mom said frantically.

"Well, come on into my office, Mrs. Zombie," he said as he took a quick glance my way with a strange look on his face.

When we got in his office, it had a bunch of Zombie clown pictures on the wall which really creeped me out.

"Now, what seems to be the problem?" the doctor asked.

"Well, my son Zombie is kind of going through some…um…changes," she said to the doctor and then she gave him a look like if he would know what she was talking about.

24

"Oh, OK. Well, let's take a look under here, why don't we?" He pulled the nylon stocking off of my head.

"Whoa! That has got to be the brightest red face I have ever seen! You must be the first in history. I've never seen anything so strange! Oh, I need to take a picture of this to show my golf buddies!"

Then the doctor ran out of the office to get his camera.

My mom slapped her face like Steve did. I guess her butt must hurt too.

Then my mom gave me a crooked smile to try to cheer me up.

It didn't really help.

She's a Zombie. She always has a crooked smile.

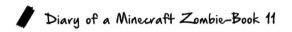

"It'll be OK, Zombie, I promise," she said.

All of a sudden the doctor came in with a few of the other nurses.

"Oh my! He is red!" one nurse said.

"He looks like a lollipop! I could just lick his head right now," another nurse said.

"That boy's head is redder than the ball at Scarget. You should talk to them you know. You could make great money doing their commercials... Or just standing in front of the store..."

Next thing I know my face was glowing redder than ever before.

SHHIINNNEE!!*

"Whoa!" the doctor and nurses said. Then they put on sunglasses and started clapping.

"WAAAAHHHHHHHHHHH!!!!!!" I started crying.

"Well I never!" My mom said as she grabbed her things and put the green nylon stocking back on my head.

I cried myself to sleep that night.

For the next 20 years I was going to be known as "Tomato Face" or "Carrot Top" or "Mooshroom Boy."

And I will never be able to see my beautiful green face ever again…

27

Wednesday

"**M**OOOOOMMMMMMMMM!!!!!!"

"What is it dear?!!!!"

My mom ran into my room.

"Look at my face!"

"Oh dear."

"Francis!"

"What is it? My dad asked, as he ran into my room.

"Oh boy."

When I looked in the mirror, now my face was all BLUE!

"WAAAHHHH!!! What's the matter with me?!!!! WAAAHHHH!!!"

"Well, Zombie, they call it mood skin because your skin usually reflects whatever mood you are in," my Dad said. "When I was younger, I used to be afraid a lot, so my skin turned…"

"WAAAHHHH!!! MOM, DO SOMETHING!!!! WAAAHHHH!!!"

All of sudden my skin started glowing a bright blue.

SHHIINNNEE!!*

"Whoa. Zombie, calm down. Don't worry, son, it will get better in time."

She looked at my Dad with a serious expression like he would know what she meant.

I knew what she meant! 20 years of misery!

"WAAAHHHH!!!"

"I think I know what will help," my Dad said. "I'll be right back."

Then he ran out of the room, out the front door and drove off.

"Mom, I can't go to school like this! The kids will laugh at me!"

"Don't worry, Zombie, it's only a phase," she said, but I could tell that she didn't really believe what she was saying.

"WAAAHHHH!!!"

A little while later my Dad came back home.

He pulled out a bag, and out of the bag my Dad pulled out some yellow tinted sunglasses and put them on. Then he gave a pair to my Mom. Then he put the last pair on my face.

"How about now, son?" he asked. "Good as new, right?"

I know parents mean well. But sometimes I just think they don't have a clue.

But at least when I looked in the mirror, I looked like my nice green self again.

I decided all this drama was just too much for me, so I went back to sleep.

As I closed my eyes, I started thinking that nobody at school is gonna be wearing yellow tinted sunglasses.

I started getting really scared about what the kids would say...

Thursday

"Mooooommmmmmmmm!!!!!!"

"What is it dear?!!!!"

My mom ran into my room.

"Look at my face!"

"Oh dear."

"Francis!"

"What is it? My dad asked, as he ran into my room.

"Oh boy."

"Dad, what did you do to me?!!!!!!"

When I looked in the mirror, my face was bright yellow!

"Dad, those glasses you gave me made me yellow!"

"Honey, I don't think it was the glasses," Mom said. "The glasses only make things look yellow. Your skin is changing because of what you're feeling."

"Looks like you were feeling really scared last night, huh Zombie?" Dad asked.

"Mmm hmmm," I said, thinking about how the kids would laugh at me at school.

"Yeah, yellow was the color that I turned when I was younger. I was a really scared kid most of my young years," Dad said, trying to make me feel better.

"Really?"

"Yep, they used to call me all kinds of names, like Chicken, Yellow Belly, Dandy-Lion, Sponge Pants, Square Bob, Ozzie-Lot,

33

Tweety-Butt, Corn on the Cob, Cheese head, Chuck…"

"Francis, that's not helping!" Mom interrupted.

But I couldn't help thinking about how the kids at school would make fun at me.

All of a sudden I started glowing brighter and brighter.

SHHIINNNEE!!*

"Whoa, Zombie, calm down. It's going to be OK, I promise," my mom said.

But I couldn't help thinking about what all the kids would say.

Friday

Schools almost here, and I'm going to have to go to school looking like a sunflower.

I know what's going to happen: they're going to laugh at me, and call me names, and point their fingers, and make fun, and chase me down the hall with pitch forks and torches...

It's going to be so embarrassing…

RRRIIIINNNGGG!!!!

All of a sudden my alarm clock rang.

Wuzzatt?

Huh?!!

Oh man! It was all a dream!

I just laid in my bed feeling so relieved. The whole thing was all a dream!

I couldn't believe it! The mood skin, and the doctor's office, and the jokes, and the finger pointing, and the pitch forks and the torches…

It was all a dream!

I was so happy that all I could do was just lie in bed and smile from ear to ear. It was the biggest smile I had ever put on my face. I had never felt this happy before.

After a little while, I got up and ran to the bathroom to gaze upon my beautiful green face, when…

"MOOOOOMMMMMMMMM!!!!!!"

"What is it, dear?"

My mom ran into my room.

"LOOK AT MYER FAISH!"

"Oh dear."

"Francis!"

"What is it? My dad asked, as he ran into my room.

"Oh boy."

"MY FAISH… I HAF… TROLL FAISH!"

All of a sudden, there was a knock on the front door.

"Don't worry, honey," Mom said, tapping my hand but looking nervous. "You'll be OK."

My mom ran down to answer the door.

"Oh, hey Steve," Mom said. "C'mon in… Yes, Zombie's upstairs. But he's going through some…um…changes."

Then I heard Steve run up the stairs.

"Whoa! It's Troll Face!"

"WAAAARRRRRHHHH!"

I tried to cry, but I couldn't keep my face from smiling.

"STEEF HELF ME!

"Uh, OK. Mr. and Mrs. Zombie, what happened?"

"Well, Zombie started to change color these past couple of days," my mom said. "Monday he was red, Wednesday he was blue, yesterday he was yellow and now today… Well…he's that."

"I see," Steve said.

"We thought he had mood skin. That's when his skin changes colors if he is feeling really intense feelings."

"I see," Steve said. Then he asked me, "So, Zombie, what were you feeling Monday?"

"I waf mad."

"I see. How about Wednesday?"

"I waf sad."

"I see. How about yesterday?"

"I waf scared."

"So when you're mad you turn red; when you're sad, you turn blue; and when you're scared you turn yellow... Hmm…" Steve said thinking to himself.

"SUMBUDY HELF ME!!!"

"I got it!" Steve said. "We just need to get Zombie to feel something that will turn him green again."

"But what feeling is going to make him turn green?" Dad asked.

"How about disgust? Whenever I'm grossed out I usually turn green," Steve said.

40

"Let's give it a try," Dad said. "So Zombie, what grosses you out?"

I tried to think but my face started to hurt because it was frozen in Troll Face position.

"We're going to have to try some different things," Steve said. "I'll be back."

Then Steve ran out of the house.

"Oh Zombie, I'm so sorry you're going through this," Mom said.

But, all I could think about was how scared I was about what the kids in school were going to say.

Oh man, I better not think about that or I'm going to turn yellow again.

Then I started getting sad because I thought I was going to be stuck like this forever.

41

Oh man, I better not think about that either or I'm going to turn blue.

Then I started getting mad. *Why is this happening to me?!!!* I thought.

Oh man, I better not think about that or I'm going to turn red.

I got so tired from all the drama that I just decided to go to sleep.

A little while later, next thing I know, the nastiest smell I had ever smelled overpowered my nose hole.

It smelled like a cross between minty fresh, dentist breath, and lilac old people smell, BLECH!

The smell was so strong I couldn't stay asleep.

When I woke up, I saw my dentist, my grandma and my grandpa standing over me. They were all out of breath.

Then everybody around me started smiling.

"What are you guys smiling about?" I said as I stuck my fingers in my nose hole.

"Take a look," Dad said.

Then he handed me a mirror.

"YEAHHHHHHHH!!!!!" I yelled as I threw my hands into the air. My beautiful green face was back!

Then all of a sudden, Dad got a real serious look on his face.

"Oh boy."

I looked at the mirror again…

"WAAAAARRRRRHHHH!!!!!!!!!!"

43

Saturday –
A Few Weeks Later...

Well, my Troll face finally went away.

When my Mom and Dad wouldn't let me be part of the next All Day Minecraft Marathon PVP Tournament that just wiped the smile right off my face.

Yeah, I had a few more color changes over the past few days.

Let me see, I was orange, and purple, and pink, and black, and magenta. There was fuchsia, which I still don't understand. And I even had a polka dot day...yeah that was a really confusing day.

But the good thing was that after a few more color changes, it just suddenly stopped.

Yeah, I guess my Mom and Dad had it all wrong.

Mood skin does eventually go away if you just bottle all your feelings up real good.

At least that's what Old Man Jenkins told me.

Old Man Jenkins came by the house yesterday to bring us some sour milk his Zombie cow made.

"Hey, there, everyberdy? Howr' the chickens kicking?"

"Oh, hello Mr. Jenkins. Thank you for the sour milk," Mom said. "Zombie is not feeling like himself today."

"Whoa there young man! What in tarnation happened to you?"

"I've got mood skin," I said.

"Mood skin huh? I haven't seen a rainbow like that, even in a bag of Skittles."

Yeah, I guess I was feeling a bunch of mixed feelings that morning.

"Let me go put this milk away," Mom said. "Mr. Jenkins, please tell Zombie how this is just a phase and that everything is going to be OK."

Then, before she left the room she gave Old Man Jenkins a look like he would know what she meant.

"Iz your Mom OK? She looked a bit constipated," Mr. Jenkins said. "At least that's what I look like when I'm constipated."

"WAAAAHHHH!!!!!"

"There, there. Don't worry about it, Zombie… It'll be alright."

"I don't want to look like a bag of Skittles for the rest of my life, Mr. Jenkins. WAAAAHHHH!!!!!"

"Well, Zombie, if you really want to lick your mood skin, you've got to bottle up your feelings really tight inside."

"What do you mean, Mr. Jenkins?"

"Well, whenever you start feeling something really strong, just clench your butt cheeks real tight, and then push all your feelings in. Like holding a fart when a pretty girl walks by."

I was never really good at holding in a fart when a pretty girl walked by. Actually, I had the opposite experience.

"Like this," Old Man Jenkins said as he clenched his butt cheeks and made a really weird face.

"HHHHHHHMMMMMMPPPPHHHH!!!!" he said, looking really intense.

Next thing you know…

BRRT, BRAAAH, THPPTPHTPHPHHPH!

PHHHHHHRT, PPPPPPPPPPPPPPPPPPPPPPPPPPP!

PFF…PRTRTRTRGURTRUFNASUTUTUTUT… PRRRT!

PFFT… PHHHHHH!

"Uh… You OK Mr. Jenkins?"

"SPLPLPLLLP!

*WHOOOOOFFFF… POOT…
PRRRRRRRVT… SCRAEFT…
PPPPPPWWARRRRPPPPP!*

*PLLLLLLLLLLLLLLLLLOOOOOOOOOOOAAA…
RRRRRRRIIIIIIIIIIIIIIIIIIIIIIIIIPPPPP!*

FUUUUUUUUUUUURRRRRRRT!

*THHHPPBBBB…
VERRRRRRRRRNNNNNNTTTTTT!*

"Uh… You want me to call a doctor for you,
Mr. Jenkins?"

HOOOOOOOOOOOOOOOOOOOOONK!
PBPBPBPBP!

FRR… FRR… FRRRRRR…RAMPOOOOOAG…
PPPPPPPPTTTTTTTTTTTTTTTTTT!

"UGH, I think this is the big one…"

FLURPPPPPPPPPPPPPPPPPPPPPPPPPPPPPPPPPP
PPTTTTTTT!

"AAAAAHHHHH!" Mr. Jenkins said, looking relieved.

"Wooooooh, sorry about that, Zombie. I think the wife put a little too much sour milk in my cereal this morning."

"Uh… That's OK, Mr. Jenkins."

But I could tell after that explosion that Mr. Jenkin's seemed a little lighter on his feet.

"I think I'll leave you to it then… Seeya, Zombie." Mr. Jenkins said as he skipped out of the room.

"PFFFTT…"

Man, I wonder if what Mr. Jenkins said will work.

Heh, it couldn't hurt, I thought.

So I squeezed my butt cheeks really tight and I put my best constipated face on… Then I tried to push my feelings really down deep and…

"BRRRRTTTT…"

Oh, man. It didn't work.

Then my Mom walked in.

"Whoa! Smells like Thanksgiving Dinner at Grandma's house in here!"

Then suddenly she stopped in her tracks.

"Zombie! Look at your face!!!"

"What do you mean, Mom?"

"Quick, look in the mirror!"

And there it was… A big patch of green, right on my cheek!

I couldn't believe it! Old Man Jenkins was right!

"Quick Mom, bring me some more sour milk!"

Next thing I know, I was drowning all my feelings in some sour milk.

But after it was all said and done, I was back to my beautiful green self again.

Anyway, I'm just glad that I don't have to deal with those "feelings" anymore.

That was just some really weird stuff.

Sunday

School started a few weeks ago, and some of the guys come over today to do some homework.

I hadn't gone to school yet because I was still recovering from my mood skin, so the teacher sent my homework to me through Zmail. That part at least was a sweet deal.

We didn't get much school work done though. That's because we spent the whole time plotting how we were going to join the next All Day Minecraft Marathon PVP Tournament that was happening this week.

"Dudes, how are we going to get on the Minecraft PVP Marathon on a school night?" Skelee asked. "My parents don't even burn torches on a school night. There's no way they're going to let me near a computer."

"Man, I don't know. But I gotta be on the next one," I said. "PewDiePie, and Captain Sparklez are both going to be on the one this week."

"Whoa," all the guys said.

"UUUUUURRRGGHHH! Why do parents have to be so mean?!" I said, really mad.

"Whoa, Zombie, don't get too mad or you're going to start changing colors again," Creepy said.

"Yeah, how did you get rid of that anyway? Slimey asked.

"I just bottled my feelings up inside," I said. "And it helps to have some sour milk around."

"Are you sure that's a good idea, Zombie?" Creepy asked. "You know, my Dad said that if you try to bottle up something as strong as feelings, then one day you could just blow up."

We all just looked at each other…Then we looked at Creepy.

"What?" Creepy asked.

"Uh… Nothing," I said.

"No seriously, he said that if you bottle all your feelings up, one day they just grow and grow and then next thing you know, your head will blow clean off and all your insides will spill out."

Then Creepy took a whiff of his Liquid Nitrogen inhaler.

KUFF, KUFF!

"Uh, Dude, I think maybe you've been using too much of that inhaler today," Skelee said.

"Naw, not my trusty inhaler. This is my secret weapon to help me deal with my feelings," he

56

said. "It's what keeps most Creeper kids from throwing tantrums."

I could tell from all of the guy's faces that we were all thinking the same thing. But we were all too chicken to ask Creepy.

Finally I got the guts to ask him.

"Uh... Creepy, what happens if a Creeper throws a tantrum?"

"Well, you remember in Science class, when the teacher said that there was a big explosion and the universe was created?"

"Wha?!!"

Later that day, I went to go find Steve to see what he was up to.

"OOOOOHHHHHMMMM. OOOOOHHHHHMMMM."

"Hey, Steve, you still doing yogurt?"

"It's Yo-ga, and yeah I am. I got really mad this morning, and I'm trying to find some inner peace."

Wow, he hasn't found that piece yet? Man, his butt must be really sore.

"What made you so mad?" I asked Steve.

"Well, I had just finished building this really cool "Man" cave yesterday, and when I came today to check it out, it was totally destroyed."

"Sounds like somebody trolled your house, dude."

"Yeah, I really put a lot of effort into that house. Urrrggggghhh!!!!"

"OOOOOHHHHHMMMM. OOOOOHHHHHMMMM."

"Hey, does that stuff really work?"

58

"It sure does. It helps me really find peace of mind."

"Dude, I lost a piece of my mind once. Me and the guys were playing a game called pencil sharpener, and I was the pencil, and…"

"OOOOOHHHHHMMMM. OOOOOHHHHHMMMM."

"Oh, OK. I get it. I guess I'll just leave you alone then."

So I said goodbye to Steve, and left him in the forest standing on his head.

I wonder why Steve just doesn't push all of his feelings inside, like Old Man Jenkins said.

Monday

"**W**AHHHHHHHHH!!!!!!

YOU'RE THE WORST!

WAHHHHHHHHH!!!!!!

PLEEEEEAAASSSEEEEEE!!!!!

WAHHHHHHHHH!!!!!!

WHY CAN'T I GO?

WAHHHHHHHHH!!!!!!

PLEASE! PLEASE! PLEASE! PLEASE! PLEASE!
PLEASE! PLEASE! PLEASE! PLEASE! PLEASE!

WAHHHHHHHHH!!!!!!

BUT WWWWHHHHHHYYYYYYYY???!!!!!

WAHHHHHHHHH!!!!!!

YOU'RE MEAN!!!!!

WAHHHHHHHHH!!!!!!"

I couldn't help it. The words just kept coming out of my mouth and I couldn't control it.

It's like my mouth was a faucet that somebody had turned on full blast.

"WAHHHHHHHHH!!!!!!"

Then my hands started flapping up and down like I was a chicken trying to fly.

Then I started jumping up and down.

Next thing I know, every bad word I had ever heard in my life started coming out of my mouth…

"L@@##$$$%!

G%^&*(#$%!

K@#$%!

N$$%%^^&&!

Z&Y%#$*@#$&*^%$@%^&*#$@^%&!

WAHHHHHHHHH!!!!!!"

"Zombie, stop throwing a tantrum this instant!" my Mom said.

But the only thing I heard coming out of her mouth was…

"NO, NO, NO!

YOU CAN'T HAVE ANY FUN!

YOU CAN'T HAVE ANY CAKE,

YOU CAN'T PLAY ANY GAMES

AND YOU CAN'T STAY UP LATE!

YOU CAN'T GO TO THE ALL DAY
MINECRAFT MARATHON PVP
TOURNAMENT AND THAT'S FINAL!"

"WAHHHHHHHHH!!!!!!"

Then my head started to hurt, and I started to
think about what Creepy said.

*"…If your feelings get too intense, one day
they just grow and grow and then next thing
you know, your head will blow clean off and
all your insides will spill out."*

So I got scared, and put on my best
constipation face on and clenched my butt
cheeks real tight. I started pushing my feelings
deep down inside, and then…

FRR… FRR… FRRRRR…RAMPOOOOOAG…
PPPPPPPPTTTTTTTTTTTTTTTTT!

Tuesday

I'm feeling a lot better today.

I don't know what happened to me yesterday.

All I know is that one minute I'm talking
to my parents about going to the All Day
Minecraft Marathon PVP Tournament, and
next thing I know I got poop in my pants.

The good thing is that I think I found another
inner piece of my spinal column, though.

My mom called it a tantrum.

It felt more like I threw up my feet out of my
mouth.

It was all because my parents wouldn't let me
be part of the All Day Minecraft Marathon
PVP Tournament.

UUURRRRGGHHH!

Why do parents have to be so mean!

I went to go see Steve again.

"OOOOOHHHHHMMMM.
OOOOOHHHHHMMMM."

Except this time, I decided to join him.

"UUUURRRGGGHHHH!
UUUURRRGGGHHHH!"

"Uh, Zombie… It's kinda hard to concentrate
with you making all that noise."

"UUUURRRGGGHHHH!
UUUURRRGGGHHHH!"

"Hey Zombie…"

"UUUURRRGGGHHHH!
UUUURRRGGGHHHH!"

"ZOMBIE!"

"UURGGHHWuzzattt?"

"Zombie, were you sleeping?"

"Oh, I guess so. Man, doing yogurt makes me
really sleepy. How was your yogurt?"

Steve stood there with that strange look on his
face.

"Forget about it. Anyway, what's going on?" Steve asked.

"Well, sometimes my parents make me so mad, I wish I was dead!"

"But you are dead."

"Wha? Awww, you know what I mean."

"Sounds like you need to find inner peace."

"Actually, now that you mention it, I found another inner piece yesterday…in my poo."

Steve just gave me that strange look again.

"I just feel like my parents never let me have any fun. You watch. One day I'm going to get really sick and die of boredom. And then they're going to feel really sorry for all of the fun things they never let me do. I can just imagine them talking now…"

MOM: "Oh Francis, I just feel like if we had only let Zombie join the All Day Minecraft

Marathon PVP Tournament he wouldn't have died of boredom."

DAD: "I know, Mildred. What were we thinking? We are such bad parents. If we had just given our baby boy everything he wanted, he would still be with us today."

I gave Steve a smug smile. "And then my ghost would haunt them for the rest of their lives. Just to remind them how sorry they should be for taking away all my fun."

"Uh…Dude, you sound like you've got some real intense feelings," Steve said. "You know, I heard that if you don't deal with your feelings, they grow and grow and eventually your head blows off and all your insides spill out."

"Wha?!! Where'd you hear that?"

"I think I heard it from some Creepers that were hanging around the 'Man' cave I was building the other day. Nice guys…Really nervous though."

"Thanks Steve, I'll see you later."

But man, I was so mad, that if I had saliva I would spit.

Then I had the best idea.

I bet if I really died of boredom then my parents would feel so sorry, that if I came back to life, they would let me do anything I wanted for the rest of my life. Even join the next All Day Minecraft Marathon PVP Tournament.

Oh man, this has got to be the best idea I have ever had.

You'll see Mom and Dad, you're going to be really sorry.

But just wait PewDiePie and CaptainSparklez. I'll see you guys at the next Tournament!

69

Wednesday

"**U**UUURRGGGHHHH!!!!"

"What is it dear?!!!!"

Mom ran into my room.

"Look at my face!"

"OH DEAR!" she cried. "FRANCIS!"

"What is it? My dad asked, as he ran into my room.

"Oh boy."

Since my parents had already seen me with a red face, blue face, yellow face, polka dot face and troll face, I had to come with something so hideous that they would really think I was dying.

So I introduced them to… ME GUSTA FACE!

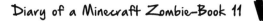

"UUUURRRGGGHHHH!!!!"

"QUICK FRANCIS, CALL THE DOCTOR!"

"Mom, I think it's too late… I think it's boredom… It's really killing me… I don't have much more time to live…. UHHHHHHHHH."

PLOP!

"FRANCIS!!! OUR SON!.... HE'S... HE'S... HE'S... DEAD!"

"Oh Mildred, what are we going to do?!!" Dad said. "How can we have been such bad parents? If we had just let him be part of the All Day Minecraft Marathon PVP Tournament, our baby boy would not have died!"

Tee hee hee. It was working! I just tried my best not to be too happy or my Troll Face would come back and spoil everything.

"OH FRANCIS, I CAN'T TAKE THIS!!! I THINK MY HEAD IS STARTING TO HURT!"

"MILDRED!"

Uh...what was going on?

"OH FRANCIS! MY HEAD! IT HURTS SO MUCH!"

"HOLD ON MILDRED, THE DOCTORS ARE COMING!"

"Mom?"

"IT BURNS! I CAN'T HOLD IT IN ANY LONGER!!!"

BOOOOMMMM!!!!!

SSSSPPLLLAAATTTTT!!!!

All of a sudden, my Mom's head blew right off, and all her insides just spilled out all over the place!

"MOM!"

All my Dad could do was just stand there crying, covered in my Mom's entrails.

"MILDRED, UURRRGGGHH!!!! DON'T WORRY, I'LL PUT YOU BACK TOGETHER! UURRRGGGHH!!!!

Then he just started sobbing and gathering all of my Mom's insides to try to stuff them back into her body.

"DAD, I'M SO SORRY! WAAAHHHH!!!! I WASN'T REALLY SICK! WAAAHHHH!!!! I WAS JUST FAKING! WAAAHHHH!!!! I DIDN'T MEAN IT! WAAAHHHH!!!!"

I just took off my Me Gusta Face Mask and stood there crying and holding my Dad while he sobbed hysterically.

He was crying so much I couldn't get him to stop.

Hey, wait a minute…

Then I looked closer and I noticed that my Dad wasn't crying… HE WAS LAUGHING!!!!

Then he just dropped Mom's corpse and started rolling around in her intestines, laughing.

I thought my Dad finally lost it and snapped. My Dad was full on crazy.

Then I heard some giggling coming from behind the closet door.

As I slowly opened the door, my Mom jumped out of the closet and fell on the floor next to Dad rolling around laughing.

"Hey, what's going on here?"

"You should've seen your face, Zombie! Hahahaha!" Dad said as he held his stomach and pointed at me.

"I didn't think I could hold it in!" Mom said, barely being able to talk because she was laughing so hard.

And there I was, just looking at both of them laughing and rolling around in my Mom's intestines.

"WWWWWWWWAAAAAAAAAAHHHH!"

"Oh, come here, Zombie. We're sorry, Honey."

"Yeah champ, He he." Dad said. "We didn't mean to laugh."

"How did you know I wasn't dead?"

"Well, first promise you won't be mad at me, Zombie," Mom said.

"Uh, OK…"

"Well, last night you feel asleep with your journal open… And I accidentally read what you wrote yesterday, and…"

"You read my journal?!!"

"I'm sorry, I couldn't help it. It was on the floor and when I picked it up it was, right there and…"

"Mom, how could you?!!!"

"I'm sorry, Zombie," Mom said with a half smile on her face. "But I bet I know how to make it up to you."

"Hmmph!"

"Well, your Dad and I were talking and we decided to let you play in the next All Day Minecraft Marathon PVP Tournament."

"What?!!! Really?!!!"

"Yes, son. We think you've been through a lot of stress lately and we wanted you to be able to have some fun to help you feel better," Dad said.

"So go and invite all your friends for a sleepover on Friday, and you can play all day and sleep in on Saturday," Mom said.

"Wow! You guys are great!"

"Come here, son," Mom and Dad said as they reached out their intestines-covered hands to give me a hug.

I was a bit grossed out…but yeah, I couldn't help it.

HUG.

Thursday

"Zombie, your friend Creepy is here to see you," Mom called out from downstairs. "And he brought a friend."

A friend? Creepy doesn't have any friends but us.

All of a sudden Creepy walked into my room.

"Sup Zombie?"

"Sup, Creeps, how you doin'?"

"Good. We miss you at school. It's not as much fun not having you there to blow something up, or to set the school on fire or something."

"Thanks," I said as I noticed this little Creeper hiding behind Creepy.

"Who's that?"

"Oh, this is my cousin Ellie. She's staying with us for a while. Her parents went to Hawaii for work. They explore volcanos so they went to check out a few new volcanos that are out there. We don't know when they'll be back."

"Uh… You better get used to her being around, Dude."

"Hi, Ellie. My name is Zack, but you can call me Zombie."

"Hi."

"What?"

"Hi...How are you?"

"Huh? I can't hear you."

"Hi...Zombie... I'm Ellie. It's nice to meet you."

I thought my Mom's prediction about losing my hearing because I had my gaming earphones on too high had come true, cause I could not hear this girl.

"Uh...OK. It's great to...err...meet you, Ellie."

"Dude, when you coming back to school?" Creepy asked.

"My Mom and Dad said since I'm OK now, I should be back on Monday. But did you hear? My Mom's gonna let me join the All Day Minecraft Marathon PVP Tournament on Friday!"

"Dude, are you serious? Hey tell your mom to call my mom. I know if your mom calls my mom, then my mom will let me go. "

"Yeah, and I'll tell my mom to call Skelee's mom and Slimey's mom," I said. "It's gonna be awesome!"

"Hey Creepy... Can I come?"

Then I heard Ellie whisper something to Creepy, but I couldn't really hear what she said.

"No, Ellie… You can't come," Creepy said.

"Why not? Pleeeaasse."

"You know why, Ellie… No way."

"Everything OK, Dude?"

"Yeah, everything's cool, Zombie," Creepy said as he left and pushed Ellie out the door. "Just make sure you tell your mom to call my mom, OK?"

"Yeah, no problem Creeps."

Hmm. That was weird.

But I'm glad that Ellie couldn't make it. This is gonna be our first All boys, All Day Minecraft Marathon PVP Tournament. And it's going to be epic.

I wouldn't want a girl messing it all up.

Friday

"**U**UUURRGGGHHH!"

"Why do I keep losing!"

SLAM!

"Whoa, Zombie, calm down. You're going to break your controller if you keep slamming it on the table like that," Skelee said.

"Yeah, Zombie. What gives?" Slimey asked me.

"I don't know. I just get so mad sometimes I just want to break this whole game! UUUURRGGGHHH!"

"Dude," Creepy said. "I know it's Minecraft PVP and all, but remember what my Dad said. If you get too intense about stuff, your

83

head is gonna blow clean off and your insides are going to spill out."

I just looked at Creepy with a disgusted look on my face. I think he felt my stare burning a hole into his head.

"What?" Creepy asked.

"Nothing." I said. "I just can't get it. I keep trying but I just keep losing! UUUURRGGGHHH! I hate this!"

"Are you kids ok up there? What's all that banging?" my mom yelled from downstairs.

"YEAH MOM, WE'RE FINE!"

"Dude, if you keep getting mad, your Mom is gonna come up here and tell us all to go to sleep," Skelee said. "Then there goes our all day marathon."

"Zombie, why don't you try my Liquid Nitrogen inhaler?" Creepy said. "It always makes me feel better."

Something inside told me that maybe it wasn't a good idea.

"Or maybe you can try my Extra Strength Natural Methane Gas inhaler. This one really calms me down when I'm feeling anxious."

Well, I didn't want to spoil our first all day marathon. But I just couldn't understand why I kept losing. UUUURRGGGHHH! It just made me so mad that I was losing to a bunch of noobs online.

"Uh… Sure," I said.

"Zombie, maybe that's not such a good idea," Slimey said.

"Eh, what's the worst that can happen? Give me that thing."

KUFF, KUFF!

"Naw, you need to take a lot more," Creepy said. "Really breathe it in."

"Uh… OK."

KUFF, KUFF, KUFF, KUFF!

In the beginning, nothing seemed to be happening. Then, all of a sudden… I started feeling really weird.

"OH man! Look at Zombie's face!"

"Whoa!" All the guys said.

"WAF WRUNG WIF MY FAISH?" I asked. "WAF WRUNG WIF MY VOISH?"

Then the guys handed me a mirror.

"Wha?!!!!!"

"UH MAN, WAT AM I GUNNA DO?"

My face felt like somebody took my head and put it in a slushy machine.

"Whoa Zombie, you look like my grandpa does when he hasn't gone to the bathroom in a week," Slimey said.

"Hey boys? You want some snacks?" My Mom asked from downstairs. "I'll bring some up for you in a minute."

"OH NO! MY MUM IS CUMBING UB DA STARS! WAT AM I GUNNA DO?"

"Hey, maybe the Liquid Nitrogen inhaler will counteract the effects, right Creepy?" Skelee asked.

"I don't know. I've never taken them both on the same day before," Creepy said.

"You boys dressed? I'm coming up," my Mom said.

"Quick Zombie, take the Liquid Nitrogen Inhaler!" Skelee said. "And make sure you take a lot this time."

So I ran into the bathroom.

"Hi boys, having a good time?" My mom asked as she walked into my room.

88

"Yes, Mrs. Zombie."

"Hey, where's Zombie?"

Something in the guy's faces must have given away that something was wrong.

"He's in the bathroom, Mrs. Zombie," Creepy said, giving me up.

"Zombie! Are you OK?!" My Mom said as she knocked on the bathroom door.

"I'M FERN!"

"Why do you sound weird? Zombie, let me in there right now!"

KUFF, KUFF, KUFF, KUFF, KUFF, KUFF, KUFF, KUFF!

"Zombie!"

"YER MOM?!"

"Zombie, open the door this instant!"

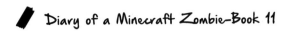
So I decided to open the door.

"Is everything OK?" my mom asked me.

"Everything is fine, Mom," I said feeling totally normal.

"Oh… OK. Well, I brought some snacks. I even got you some of your favorite cake."

All of a sudden my head started to feel weird.

"Mom, I think my head is starting to hurt."

"Really funny, Zombie," Mom said.

"BUT MOM! MY HEAD! IT HURTS SO MUCH!"

"Nice try, young Zombie," Mom said. "That joke was already perfected by your Dad and I."

"MOM, IT BURNS! I CAN'T HOLD IT IN ANY LONGER!!!"

"Son, I think you're going to need some acting lessons before you'll pull one over on me," Mom said.

"Uh… Mrs. Zombie, I think something's really wrong with Zombie," Slimey said, pointing at my expanding cranium.

"Ha! I see you got your minions in on the joke too, huh," Mom said. "But it's getting kind of old and…"

BOOOOOOOOOOOOOMMMM!!!!!

SSSSPPPPPLLLAAATTTTT!!!!

91

Saturday –
A Few Weeks Later...

"**U**uuuuh! My head…"

Steve was in my room standing over me.

"Oh… Hey Steve. Whatcha doing here?"

"Dude, how're you feeling?" Steve asked me.

"I got a really bad headache, and my neck hurts, and my stomach hurts, and… What happened?"

"Well, the guys told me that you were really mad and your head blew clean off, and all your insides spilled out."

"WHATTTT?!!! SERIOUSLY?!!!!"

"Yeah, it took us weeks to find your head. It had blown right through the roof of your house and it landed in my village."

All of a sudden I noticed something sticking out of my face.

"What's this on my face?"

"Well, I got some good news and I got some bad news. Which one do you want to hear first?"

"What's the bad news?"

"Well, your head landed right outside of the nose doctor's office in my village and..."

"GET ME A MIRROR, QUICK!"

"Yeah, he couldn't help himself," Steve said. "...Say hello to your new nose."

93

"WAAAAHHHH! LOOK AT MY FACE! WAAAAHHHH!"

"Whoa, Zombie, calm down. You're going to blow your head off again if you don't chill out."

BURRRRRRRR! SQUISH! BURRRRRRRR! SQUISH!

"What's that sound?" I asked . "And why does my stomach hurt?"

"Well, they had a hard time finding all of your insides," Steve said. "But the doctor said they would eventually grow back. I just thought you would feel better if you at least had something inside you to keep you warm."

I lifted up my shirt, and something flopped out and fell on the floor.

SPLAT!

"Hold on, I'll help you put it back in," Steve said. "I guess that duct tape didn't hold as good as I thought."

"WHAT IS THAT?!!!"

"Well, they say that squid feels just like intestines, so I thought you would feel better if you at least had something inside of you."

95

"Why does my neck hurt?"

"Well, that was the tricky part. The doctor said since they couldn't find your head, then they would try to get you a new one. But they had a hard time finding one your size because you're so small for your age."

Figures, I thought.

"I just thought you would be much happier with your old head so, it took me a few weeks, but I found it."

"Where was it?"

"Aw man, your head had been halfway around the world and back before I found it. Let me see... After the nose doctor, it went to a witch doctor, and then it got shipped overseas and they put it in a museum. And then somebody stole it, and then it was sold on the black market, and next thing you know, a few weeks later, I found it on EBay."

"EBAY?!!!"

"Yeah, it cost me a whole fourteen dollars and twenty cents. I was the highest bidder."

As he was talking I felt my neck, and it felt like metal.

"Yeah, I didn't really trust the doctor much, so I put your head back on myself. I tried

97

duct tape at first, but your head kept leaning toward the side. Then I tried glue, but I couldn't keep it in place so your head kept sticking to your shoulder. Finally, I used a stapler and..."

"A STAPLER?!!!" I felt around my neck and it felt like I had spikes all the way around.

"Why does it feel weird?"

"Well, I didn't think you would like the stapler look so I added a special collar to give you a cooler vibe."

"UUHHHH! So what's the good news?"

"Uh… I think you're married."

"WHATTTTTTT?!!!!!!"

"Yeah, Um… Creepy felt really bad for what happened to you so he came by a lot to take care of you."

"So?"

"Well, sometimes Creepy couldn't make it, so sometimes he would send Ellie to come by and take care of you and…"

"Oh Man."

"Yeah, I found some selfies she was keeping under your bed and, well, uh… Take a look."

"Wha?!!!"

"You know, I was wondering why she kept taking your body outside..."

"Wha? I'm married?!!!! I'm only 13 years old!"

Steve just stood there looking at me.

All of a sudden...

"PFFFFFFFTTTTT!!!! HAHAHAHAHA!"

Steve started rolling around on the floor laughing.

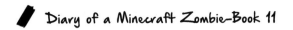

"Man, you should've seen the look on your face! HAHAHAHAHA!"

Then he came over to me and took my nose off, and then he took the spiked collar off.

"Those were fake?!!!"

"Yeah, you don't have staples either," Steve said.

I touched my neck and it was perfectly fine.

"But I think you're still married…"

"Wha?!!!"

"Just kidding. But I think that Ellie has a real crush on you, man. She really took a liking to your corpse."

"Man, I'm gonna get you!"

I tried to jump out of bed, but my head was still hurting real bad.

"Hey, why does my head still hurt?"

"Well, it wasn't true that I got your head on Ebay. I actually found it on the school soccer field, nearby," Steve said. "Well, me and the guys were kinda bored from looking for your head, so we decided to have a quick soccer game, and...uh... we didn't have a ball, and...uh... Your head was the perfect size and..."

Wow, with friends like these, who needs enemies...?

Sunday

My head still hurt from Steve and the guys' soccer ball game.

But I'm just glad that all that drama is over.

I mean, why do we need to deal with our feelings anyway?

I still like Old Man Jenkin's idea of squeezing your butt cheeks and pushing your feelings deep inside.

Except nowadays, I can't do it as much.

The doctor said I have a weak stomach.

It hasn't fully grown back since I lost it.

Creepy came by to see me this morning.

It was really weird because Ellie was with him.

I didn't know what to say to her, especially because there was a chance that we were married.

"Sup, Zombie, how you feeling today?"

"I feel alright," I said, trying not to look at Ellie. She's always hiding behind Creepy so it wasn't that hard.

"Hey, what are these pictures on the floor?" Creepy said picking up my Ellie pics.

Oh man, I forgot to put those away!

After Creepy looked at them, I could tell he didn't know about Ellie taking me out on our field trips.

I felt really bad for Ellie, though. Creepy just looked at her with a surprised look on his face.

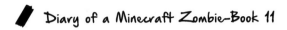

Then Ellie burst out crying and ran out the door.

Oh, Man. More drama.

All of a sudden Creepy started getting anxious. He pulled out his inhaler and took a couple of whiffs from it.

KUFF, KUFF!

"Dude, don't worry about it man, it was just some pictures," I told Creepy.

"It's not that, Zombie. It's that… Well… Ellie is really, really shy. It's because she doesn't like to feel embarrassed," Creepy said.

"Man, I can relate."

"Well, one time when Ellie was little, she accidentally farted at my birthday party. She got so embarrassed she locked herself in the bathroom for a whole day."

106

"What's wrong with that?"

"Well, Ellie is allergic to inhalers, so...well... uh...remember when I told you about how the universe started with a big explosion?"

"Uh huh,"

"Well, let's just say that there wasn't a canyon in Ellie's village before her family moved there."

Oh man… More drama.

Thursday

*"**Y**es, we are getting reports that the Zombie National Guard has been called in to provide support to the Zombie Army and the Navy. They have quarantined the house, but it may be in vain. Preliminary reports coming in say that if the E.L.E does explode, it will end the Minecraft World as we know it. We'll have more news for you at 11. And now the weather...."*

Oh man, things are getting really serious over at Creepy's house.

It's been 4 days and Ellie is still locked in Creepy's bathroom.

Creepy and his family have been staying with us for a few days since the Zombie Army took over his house.

And it's been a lot of work just trying to keep them calm.

I sure didn't want an explosion at my house... Especially since I just finished rebuilding my booger collection.

All the guys and Steve came over to my house to check out what was happening.

"Hey Creeps, you doing OK?" Skelee asked.

"Oh man, oh man, oh man, oh man, oh man..." Creepy said anxiously.

"Whoa, calm down Creeps, we don't want the Army coming over here," Skelee said.

"Yeah Creepy, can you take a few puffs of your Liquid Nitrogen inhaler to calm down?" Slimey asked.

"He ran out yesterday," I said. "He's using his Natural Methane Gas inhaler now."

"Dudes! You know what that means…" Steve said pulling out a match.

"FART LIGHTING!"

"No way!" All the guys said.

"Yeah Steve, you think Ellie is bad, Creepy's farts will blow us right into the next village."

"Oh OK. I just thought I would lighten up the mood a little bit."

"Oh man, oh man, oh man, oh man, oh man…" Creepy kept saying.

KUFF, KUFF!

"So what are we gonna do about Ellie?" Skelee asked. "They say on the news that she could go nuclear any minute."

"Zombie, I think if you talk to Ellie, she'll calm down," Steve said.

"Not now bro," I tried to say under my breath, making a face that I knew Steve would understand.

"Dude, what's going on between you and Ellie?" Skelee asked.

"Yeah Zombie, are you guys a couple?" Slimey asked.

"Actually, I think Zombie and Ellie are married," Steve said. "Check out the pictures."

Then Steve started handing out my Ellie pics to all the guys.

"Steve, those are private! Uh… I mean… Those are for me only… I mean… Oh… I don't know what I mean!"

"Whoa, Zombie, you guys look like you're really in LLLUUUUUUUVVVVV!"

"Stop it! That's not funny."

"Zombie, I bet if you talk to Ellie, she'll calm down," Steve kept saying.

"Me?!!! I don't even know Ellie that well!"

"Well, from these pictures, it looks like she knows you REALLY good… PFFFFFFFFFTTTTT!"

Then all the guys started laughing.

"Zombie, please help Ellie," Creepy said with a sad look on his face. "You're the only one that could do it."

"Oh alright, I'll do it. But if I do this, it stays between all of us, OK?"

"Sure… Yeah… No problem, Dude."

Something told me by the end of the week everybody in school is gonna know about it.

"And give me those pictures!"

112

SNATCH.

"I'm putting these away so only I can see them... I mean... So no one can see them but me... I mean..."

"Oooooooooooh!"

"UUUURRRRGGGGHHH!"

Thurday Night

"**W**ell, folks, this is it. We just got a report that there is a large spike of radiation build up coming from the residence of the Creepers on Pixelcraft Street. We have been informed that a few more spikes of this magnitude from the E.L.E. and it's the end of the Minecraft world as we know it. More information after a word from our sponsors..."

"Hey, they're talking about Ellie on the news!" I said.

"Naw, their talking about ELE," Steve said.

"That's what I said, Ellie!"

"No, they're talking about ELE," Steve said again.

"We're all talking about Ellie, right?" Skelee asked.

"No we're talking about ELE," Steve said.

"Aren't we going to go help Ellie?" Slimey asked.

"Yes, we are going to help Ellie, because she's an ELE," Steve said.

My head started to hurt talking to Steve and the guys about Ellie.

"You guys don't know what an ELE is, do you?" Steve said with a look of *Duh* on his face.

All the guys just looked at each other like we had fallen through a Nether Portal.

"An E-L-E is an Extinction Level Event, meaning if we don't calm Ellie down, it won't just be the neighborhood she's gonna blow up, it'll be every neighborhood."

"Whoa!"

All of a sudden everybody got really scared about dealing with ELE… I mean Ellie… I mean Ellie the ELE…UURRRGGHH!

"Alright guys, gear up! We need to get into Creepy's house and then find a way to talk some sense into that little creeper."

"Don't you mean your little ' *love creeper*'?" Steve said.

Then all the guys started laughing again.

"Hey, I'm serious. I don't even know if Ellie is going to listen to me. So let's do this!"

"How are we supposed to get into Creepy's house anyway? The Army has the place surrounded," Slimey asked.

"We can get in through the mineshaft that runs under my house," Creepy said.

"Sometimes I get really lonely and go down there looking for some diamond miners to make friends with."

"OK, so, I'll distract her, while you guys come from behind and put the bag over her head. Slimey, did you bring your Dad's Sunday pants like I told you?"

"Yup, all ready. It was hard getting them off of him, but I did it."

I really did not know what to say to that… I was just glad that Slimey's Dad is the biggest Slime in the neighborhood… And his pants were huge.

"Alright guys, let's do this!"

Thursday – Late Night

"**D**ude, this mineshaft is boss! I just found an emerald over there," Steve said.

"Yeah, I found some cake somebody left behind too," Slimey said.

"Hey guys, we don't have time for fun. Creepy, how do we get into your house?"

"There's a ladder up ahead that leads right into my bathroom."

"Your bathroom? Hey wait a minute, isn't Ellie hiding in your bathroom?" I asked.

"Yeah, what about it?" Creepy asked.

I just looked at Creepy. He probably felt the hole burning into his head from my stare.

"Forget it. Alright, so I'll sneak in there and distract her, and you guys grab her from behind. But be quiet. We don't want to scare her, or that's it, game over."

"So I guess you're going first, lover boy?" Steve asked.

"Uuurrrggghh!" I said under my breath.

So we reached the ladder, but when we looked up, we just saw a bright green flashing glow coming from Creepy's bathroom.

"Alright Zombie, do your thing," Steve said… "And don't forget to get on one knee…and make sure you have the ring."

"Ha… You got jokes," I said as I gave Steve my best Me Gusta Face look.

So I climbed up the ladder all the way to the top.

119

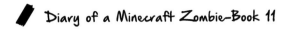

"How's it looking up there?" Steve yelled.

I was in such shock that all I could do was climb down.

"Uh… Dudes… I think we're gonna need a bigger bag," I said.

Thursday –
Late, Late Night

"**W**hat's up, Zombie?"

"Go take a look," I said.

Then everybody climbed up the ladder.

"Whoa!"

"So how are we going to help her now?"
Skelee asked.

Ellie was now about 100 feet tall, she was
sticking out of the top of the house, and she
was pulsating with a bright green glow.

"Zombie, you're going to have to get up there and talk her down," Steve said.

"How am I supposed to do that?"

Then Steve just smiled at me, and he gave me a look like I would know what he meant.

"It's that time," he said with a big smile on his face.

"What time?" I asked, not knowing what in the world he was talking about.

Then Steve just grabbed my head and turned it toward Creepy.

Then I got it.

So I walked over to Creepy.

"Uh… Hey, Creepy, can I borrow your Natural Methane Gas Inhaler?"

"Yeah, sure Zombie. Knock yourself out. You feeling anxious?"

"No, I'm OK. A little grossed out with myself right now, but I'm OK."

"Alright everybody, stand back!" Steve said. "Zombie, take as much as you can… Empty the bottle if you have to."

So I grabbed the inhaler, put it to my mouth and…

KUFF, KUFF, KUFF, KUFF, KUFF, KUFF, KUFF, KUFF, KUFF, KUFF, KUFF, KUFF, KUFF, KUFF, KUFF…Kefff!

"Alright, it's empty. Cough, cough."

"Here it goes," Steve said as he took out a match and lit it. "Do it, Zombie!"

So I squeezed my butt cheeks together, and took all my feelings and buried them down deep. And then I put on my best constipation face and…

"BRRRRT."

BOOOOOOOOOOOOOOOOMMMMMM!!!!!!

I went flying in the air so fast I think I left my butt behind.

It seemed like a good idea at the time, but now I had to find a place to land.

But I didn't have to worry about that because at that moment, Ellie turned her head so I smacked right into her lips.

"THAT'S IT LOVERBOY!" Steve yelled. "MAKE US PROUD!!!!"

I could hear all the other guys cheering, yelling and laughing down below.

I pulled myself out of her pucker, and jumped on the top of a tall tree she was standing next to.

"ELLIE!!!" I yelled.

Ellie turned in my direction, and when she recognized it was me, she got really shy and took a few steps backward to hide behind another tall tree.

I think she crushed like half a dozen tanks down on the ground.

"ELLIE!!! IT'S OK. IT'S ME, ZOMBIE! I WANT TO TALK TO YOU!"

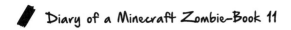
Ellie still wouldn't come out from behind the tree.

"ELLIE, I THINK THE PICTURES WERE GREAT! I JUST WANTED TO SAY THANK YOU FOR BEING SO NICE TO ME WHEN I WAS SICK."

Then Ellie started to walk toward my tree. She crushed another half a dozen tanks while walking toward me.

"Uh… Sorry Army guys down there."

Ellie got up really close to me, so I stepped onto her shoulder.

I really didn't know what to say. I really didn't think I would get that far.

So I said the first thing that came to my mind.

I got down on one knee, and whispered in her ear…

"Uh, Ellie… Will you… Uh… Marry me?"

All of a sudden, Ellie started glowing faster and faster and faster.

Oh man, instead of helping her, I think I made it worse. Ellie was about to blow!

So, I jumped.

I landed right on top of Creepy's house. Then I saw the guys below.

"GUYS, RUN! SHE'S ABOUT TO BLOW!!!"

All the guys took off.

Ellie started flashing and glowing faster, and faster, and faster and faster…

Then I took a huge jump off the roof… And suddenly…

KABBBBBOOOOOOOOOOOMMMM!!!!!

127

Friday

"**W**ake up, Zombie…"

"Zombie, wake up…"

As I opened my eyes… I could tell I was in my room again.

"How are you feeling?"

"Oh man, what happened?"

Then, I couldn't believe it...

It was Ellie standing over me!

"Hey Ellie, are you OK?"

"Yeah, I'm better now. Thanks to you."

"But the explosion? And… Where are the guys?!!!"

"We're all here, man," Steve said as he and they guys walked into my room.

"But the explosion?!! What happened?"

"Well, Zombie," Creepy said, "Thanks to you, Ellie imploded. You see when Creepers get happy they don't explode, they implode. It's how baby Creepers are normally born."

"Yeah Zombie," Steve said, "You're gonna be a father!"

"WHATTTT???!!!!"

Everybody just stood there quiet for a while, and then they just burst out laughing.

"Just kidding Dude," Steve said. "Ellie didn't implode or explode. She just shrank to her normal size so fast that she released a burst of kinetic energy that heated the molecules around her, causing them to travel faster than the speed of sound, which in turn caused a shock wave that broke the sound barrier and

129

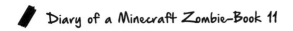
made a thundering sound like the sky was cracking open."

Everybody just looked at Steve with a stunned look on our face.

"Well, at least that's what they said on the news anyway," he said.

Well, all I know is that I just dodged a bullet. I wasn't ready to be father. But then I remembered that I asked Ellie to marry me, so I was still in a real mess.

"Zombie, thank you for helping me," Ellie said. And then she stooped down and whispered in my ear. "And don't worry about what you said. I know you only said it to help me. So, I won't tell if you won't."

Wow, Ellie was cool. Really cool. I'm still kinda creeped out about her stalker pics, but I think I can get used to her being around.

Then my Mom walked into my room.

"Who wants cake?" Mom asked.

"YEAH!!!"

"And there's plenty more downstairs. You're going to need all the energy you can get for your All Day Minecraft Marathon PVP Tournament today."

"Are you serious?" I said as my Mom stood there smiling.

"AW-YEAH! Let's do this!"

"Hey Creepy, can I stay?" Ellie asked.

"But Ellie, if you stay, you're gonna beat us all," Creepy said. Then he looked at us and said, "Yeah, Ellie won the last 3 'Minecraft Marathon PVP Tournaments' in a row. We don't stand the chance if she stays."

Oh yeah. I think I can really get used to having Ellie around.

Saturday

Well, we had our All Day Minecraft Marathon PVP Tournament yesterday and I came in first place!

Actually, Ellie destroyed everybody else, and then she probably let me win.

Yeah, she's really cool.

I think I'm gonna ask her to come to my birthday party.

I'm gonna turn 14. But it doesn't really matter because Zombies live forever. I mean we're dead so we're dead forever... I mean... Aw, forget it.

So I learned that even though Old Man Jenkins meant well, it's probably not a good idea to bottle up all your feelings inside.

And you shouldn't ever make a constipation face. I heard that if a fly passes by, your face will get stuck like that forever.

Anyway, what I did learn is that it's better just to have a bunch of friends that you can talk to about your feelings.

And I have the best friends any Zombie could ask for.

And just in case that doesn't work, you can always try yogurt, and go find your inner piece.

"OOOOOHHHHHMMMM, OOOOOHHHHHMMMM…

UUUURRGGGHHHH… UUUURRRGGGHHHH…"

"…..ZZZZZZZZZZZZZZ!"

The End

Please Leave Us a Review

Please support us by leaving a review.
The more reviews we get the more
books we will write!

And if you really liked this book,
please tell a friend. I'm sure they will
be happy you told them about it.

Check Out Our Other Books from Zack Zombie Publishing

The Diary of a Minecraft Zombie
Book Series

Get The Entire Series on
Amazon Today!

The Ultimate Minecraft Comic Book Series

Get the Entire Series on Amazon Today!

Herobrine's Wacky Adventures

Get The Entire Series on Amazon Today!

The Mobbit

An Unexpected Minecraft Journey

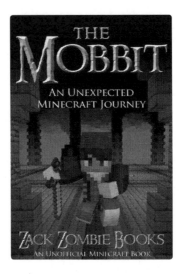

Get The Entire Series On Amazon Today!

An Interview With a Minecraft Mob

Get The Entire Series on Amazon Today!

141

Minecraft
Galaxy Wars

Get The Entire Series on
Amazon Today!

Ultimate Minecraft Secrets:

An Unofficial Guide to Minecraft Tips, Tricks and Hints to Help You Master Minecraft

Get Your Copy on Amazon Today!